poingo™
START

HIGH SCHOOL MUSICAL
Reach for the Stars

SENIOR CLASS

What's Your Passion?

A
B
C

The theater is a temple of art—a precious cornucopia of creative energy.

Gabriella Montez

Troy Bolton

I've been behind on my homework since preschool.

Give me a beat.

Everybody loves a good jazz square.

Plans for the summer: Grow, write music... grow.

Sharpay Evans

Ryan Evans

Hip-hop is my passion. I love to pop, and lock, and jam, and break....It's just dancing. Sometimes I think it's cooler than homework.

I don't really want to see my sister crash and burn... at least I think I don't.

Entertainers are so temperamental.

Martha Cox

Zeke Baylor

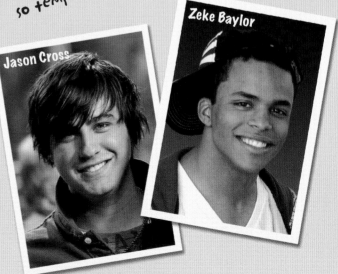

Jason Cross

What time is it, East High Seniors? Well, after four incredible years of ups and downs, smiles and frowns, it's time for the Senior Wildcats to put on their caps and gowns! But let's not forget all the incredible memories they've made during their time at East High. They've sunk baskets and sung ballads; they've run lab experiments and lay-ups. They've won championships and scholarships and made amazing lifelong friendships. What's more, they've paved the way for all current and future East High students to express who they are and reach for the stars.

I once scored 41 points on a league championship game....On the same day, I invented the space shuttle and microwave popcorn.

The team is you. You are the team.

Did you ever feel like there's this whole other person inside of you just looking for a way to come out?

Kelsi Nielsen

We exist in an alternate universe to Troy the basketball boy.

The team that washes dishes together wins together.

Chad Danforth

If you play basketball, you're going to end up on the cereal box. If you sing in musicals, you're going to end up in my mom's refrigerator.

Taylor McKessie

We're All in This Together

Crème brûlée...it's a creamy custard-like filling with a caramelized surface. It's really satisfying.

I've already picked out the colors for my dressing room.

Ms. Darbus

Coach Bolton

always liked the idea of being in charge of my own future—until it actually started happening.

BFFs!

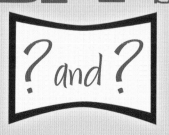
? and ?

You got game?

Check out **Team Captain** Troy's fancy footwork!

Basket

Give-and-Go

Double Dribble

BET on it

Travel

Troy's favorite way to chill out is...?

Fouled Out

Team Captain Troy Bolton rules the court, leading the Wildcats to thrilling basketball championship wins. But there's a lot more to Troy than meets the eye. No one at East High will forget when he challenged the status quo and took to center stage. Whether he's slam-dunking, golf-club-swinging, or duet-singing, Troy gives everything he does his very best shot.

Memorable Troy Friendship Moment: Serenading Gabriella to convince her to go to callbacks with him.

Wildcats

Best friends and basketball buds Chad and Troy can really tear up the court!

Chad's favorite food is...?

Chad's favorite way to chill out is...?

WILDCAT 8

What's Your Passion? A B C

TOP 10 T-shirts!

Doesn't Play Well with Others

EASILY DISTRACTED

HE DID IT

I Come With My Own Background Music

I majored in VACATION

Chad's favorite place is...?

Hey batter batter...swing!

For someone who doesn't dance, Chad is fast on his feet.

Basketball or baseball, Chad's an all-around good sport!

Chad's favorite animal is...?

Chad's favorite color is...?

Eat Sleep Slam Dunk

Laughing on the Inside

My other T-shirt is a designer one

VIVA LA BASKETBALL

I Worship Waffles

Chad Danforth is a basketball and baseball star with style. Known around East High for his snappy T-shirt slogans, he's as quick with a comeback as he is with a full-court press or a cross-field catch. In or out of play, Chad is a trustworthy teammate and true-blue friend.

Memorable Chad Friendship Moment: Accepting Troy's brotherly apology in the Lava Springs kitchen.

Zeke's favorite place is...?

He's sleek, he's chic... he's Zeke!

Zeke's favorite way to chill out is...?

What's Your Passion? A B C

Jason's favorite color is...?

Zeke's favorite food is...?

It's **hard** to **tell who's more relieved** that it's **the last day of school,** Jason or Ms. Darbus!

Looks like Zeke finally found a way to woo Sharpay!

Jason's favorite way to chill out is...?

Who can mix it up on the court and mix it up in the kitchen? Fast breaker / great baker Zeke Baylor, that's who! From cookies to crème brûlée, everything Zeke makes is magic. Teammate Jason Cross also cooks up a good time wherever he goes, thanks to his friendly and fun-loving reputation.

Memorable Jason Friendship Moment: Helping Kelsi shoot a basket after the end of the championship game.

Jason's got his head in the game.

What team? Wildcats!

Jason's favorite food is...?

SPORTS

me!

son's favorite place is...?

Zeke's favorite color is...?

Science class is Gabriella's home-away-from-home.

Not **everyone** can correct the teacher and get away **with it**!

Gabriella's favorite color is...?

GM and RE

What's Your Passion?

A
B
C

She's got a **smile** that lights **up** the stage!

Though she came to East High only two years ago as a transfer student, Gabriella Montez has more than made her mark on the Wildcats. As masterful with a math equation as she is with a melody, she always leaves the Wildcats wondering what amazing things she'll accomplish next.

Memorable Gabriella Friendship Moment: Thanking Sharpay for sharing her vocal exercise technique.

Gabriella's favorite animal is...?

Gabriella's favorite place is...?

Gabriella's favorite way to chill out is...?

Gabriella's favorite food is...?

Student: Gabriella Montez
Grade: 12
Year: 2007-2008

Absent: 0   **Tardy:** 0

EAST HIGH
HIGH SCHOOL
REPORT CARD

Proficiency	
3	Above grade level
2	At grade level
1	Below grade level

Grade Key	
A	Excellent
B	Above average
C	Average
D	Below average
F	Fail

Reading			
Overall			
Speed	A	A	A
Comprehension	3	3	3
	3	3	3

Writing			
all	A	A	A
ity	3	3	3
Strategies	3	3	3

Studies			
	A	A	A
	A	A	A

Science			
Overall	A	A	A

Mathematics			
Overall			
Problem Solving	A	A	A
Calculations	3	3	3
	3	3	3

Music			
Theory			
Performance	A	A	A
	A	A	A

Art			
Creativity	A	A	A
Understanding Concepts	3	3	3

Comments: ...s a pleasure to have in class!

JOURNAL

DIVE IN

SMILE

DIVE IN

Star Dazzle

Star Dazzle

DIVE IN

EAST HIGH SCHOOL
Name: Gabriella Montez
Class: Senior

Gabriella totes **more** than just books in **her** backpack.

Check out **her** cell phone, music player, and **more!**

(But what**ever** you do,

don't **let** Ms. Darbus catch **you** with that cell!)

animals

agriculture
life

What could brainy Taylor and the "lunkhead" basketball team possibly have to talk about?

zoology   plants

TM and GM   disease

Despite her tough talk about athletes, Taylor's a true friend to Chad.

elements

biology

the universe
beyond earth

meteorology

geology

What's Your Passion? A B C

Taylor's favorit
color is...?

Multi-tasking Taylor is on lots of school committees, but she always keeps up her great grades.

Scholastic Decathlon

Taylor McKessie is a force of nature, as well as a friend to the end. Her sharp scientific mind has led the Scholastic Decathlon Team to a blazing victory, and will undoubtedly lead to a very bright future. Teammate Martha Cox is no slouch in the science lab herself, but who would have guessed that she's just as at home on the hip-hop scene?

Memorable Taylor Friendship Moment: Showing Gabriella how to speak "cheerleader." Ohmygosh!

Martha's favorite color is...?

physics

the earth

Taylor's favorite food is...?

pathology

Don't let that shy look fool you.

weather

Pop **quiz** or **pop, lock, and jam...** Martha's got **it covered!**

farming

matter, energy, motion, and force

Martha's got **the moves!**

astronomy

botany

Martha's favorite food is...?

Martha's favorite way to chill out is...?

Taylor's favorite way to chill out is...?

chemistry

PROM...and life after high school!

TB and GM

Check 'em out...
East High's stylin' seniors are
dressed to dance the night away!

Breaking Free

Did you know...?

The East High mascot is...?

What's Your Passion?

A
B
C

The music, the dancing, the romance…hands-down, prom is the shining star of senior year. Thanks to the tireless efforts of the Prom Committee, led by Taylor McKessie, this year's senior prom was a night to remember forever. But not everyone will remember it, namely Gabriella Montez, who had to go her own way—to college—before the big night.

Memorable Prom Friendship Moment: Tux-wearing Troy turning up at Gabriella's college to dance with her on prom night.

START

Reach for the Stars

The Wildcats' top rivals are…?

The University of Albuquerque team name is…?

music ♪

?

science

basketball

drama

Fabulous!

Toodles!

Sharpay's favorite way to chill out is...?

Sharpay's favorite place is...?

Sharpay's favorite animal is...?

Sharpay's favorite food is...?

Sharpay's favorite color is...?

What can we say about Sharpay Evans that she hasn't already said about herself—many, many times? Drama Club co-president and an undisputed star of the stage, she's a determined diva who'll stop at nothing to get the part and bop to the top. Of course, she'll make sure she looks fabulous while she's doing it.

Memorable Sharpay Friendship Moment: Admitting to Zeke that the cookies he baked for her were delicious.

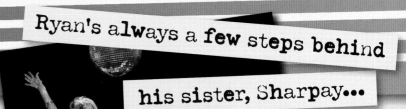
Ryan's always a **few steps behind**

his sister, Sharpay...

or is he??

Ryan's favorite food is...?

Ryan's favorite color is...?

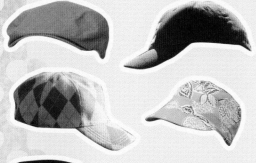

"Baseball player" isn't Ryan's **usual role**, but **when he stepped up** to the plate he **proved** that **he's got game!**

Though he's best known as his twin sister Sharpay's other half, Ryan Evans is a star in his own right. An important player in East High's theater productions, Ryan has surprised the rest of the Wildcats—and probably himself—by playing baseball, playing piano, and playing nice!

Memorable Ryan Friendship Moment: Teaching Chad and the rest of the Wildcats how to dance… during a baseball game!

DRAMA

Ryan's favorite way to chill out is...?

Kelsi

Troy

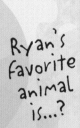

Sharpay

Ryan's favorite animal is...?

What's in a Name?

Taylor

Zeke

Ryan's favorite place is...?

Gabriella

Ryan

What's Your Passion?

A
B
C

DRAMA

Kelsi can play anywhere!

Kelsi might seem quiet, but her beautiful tunes come through loud and clear.

Kelsi's favorite place is...?

Kelsi's favorite color is...?

Kelsi's favorite way to chill out is...?

Whatever song she's working on, it's sure to be a show-stopper!